Marshal Matt
and the
Case of the
Freezing Fingers

Nancy I. Sanders
Illustrated by Larry Nolte

CPH.
SAINT LOUIS

To Jeff, with cherished memories of snowy sled rides down the hill on the farm.

Marshal Matt: Mysteries with a Value

Marshal Matt and the Slippery Snacks Mystery
Marshal Matt and the Topsy-Turvy Trail Mystery
Marshal Matt and the Case of the Secret Code
Marshal Matt and the Puzzling Prints Mystery
Marshal Matt and the Case of the Freezing Fingers

Scripture taken from the HOLY BIBLE, NEW INTERNATIONAL VERSION®. NIV®. Copyright © 1973, 1978, 1984 by International Bible Society. Used by permission of Zondervan Publishing House. All rights reserved.

Copyright © 1997 Nancy I. Sanders
Published by Concordia Publishing House
3558 S. Jefferson Avenue, St. Louis, MO 63118-3968
Manufactured in the United States of America

Library of Congress Cataloging-in-Publication Data

Sanders, Nancy I.
    Marshal Matt and the case of the freezing fingers / Nancy I. Sanders;
illustrated by Larry Nolte.
       p.   cm. —(Marshal Matt, mysteries with a value; 5)
    Summary: Marshal Matt needs Jesus' help to solve the mystery of
Janie's missing mittens.
    ISBN 0-570-04811-7
    [1. Mystery and detective stories. 2. Christian life—Fiction. 3. Lost and
found possessions—Fiction. 4. Sharing—Fiction.]
    I. Nolte, Larry, ill. II. Title. III. Series: Sanders, Nancy I.
Marshal Matt, mysteries with a value; 5.
PZ7.S19784Mak   1997
[E]—cd21   96-53870

1 2 3 4 5 6 7 8 9 10   06 05 04 03 02 01 00 99 98 97

My friends call me Marshal
Matt. I solve mysteries. Saturday
was the church sled riding party. I
solved a mystery at the party. A
cold mystery. A freezing mystery.

It all started in the barn. It wasn't cold in the barn. It was warm. Everyone drank cocoa before playing in the snow. I fed carrots to my horse, Mister E. Just then, Janie ran up. Her gray parrot, Blinky, sat on her shoulder.

"I need help," Janie said.
"Look." She held up one hand in
front of my face.

Blinky blinked. He held up one
foot, "Looky, cookie!" he squawked.
He almost fell off Janie's shoulder.

I looked at Janie's hand. "I see five fingers," I said.

"Right," Janie said. "You're supposed to see five snowmen."

"Snowmen?" I asked.

"Snowmen," Janie said. "I got new gloves. On the end of each finger is a snowman. With a black hat. The ones on the little fingers wear red hats."

Janie pointed across the barn. Her baby brother, Fred, sat on a bale of hay. Fred held a blue toy hammer in his fist. He wore a little pair of ice skates on his feet.

"I took off my gloves," Janie said. "I put them on a bale of hay. I tied the skates on Fred. Then I looked for my gloves. They were gone. Will you help me find them, Marshal Matt? Before my fingers freeze?"

Blinky blinked. He started to sing. He sang "Frosty the Snowman." Janie groaned.

I took off my gloves. I unzipped my coat. I reached into my shirt pocket. I pulled out my badge. I pinned my badge on my coat. "I, Marshal Matt, will help solve this mystery."

"Thanks," Janie smiled. She started to walk away. Then she stopped. "Wait. I'm taking Fred ice skating. What are *you* going to do? Build a snowman for the contest?"

"No. I'm going sled riding. Down the big hill."

"How will I know if you find the gloves?" Janie asked. "How will you know if I find the gloves?"

I reached into my coat pocket. I pulled out a piece of paper. It was from Sunday school. A Bible verse was on it. It said: *Do not forget to do good and to share with others. Hebrews 13:16.*

I turned the paper over. I pulled out a white crayon and a green marker. I, Marshal Matt, knew what to do.

"Secret messages," I whispered.

"Secret messages?" Janie whispered.

Blinky blinked. "Want to hear a secret?" he squawked.

Everyone turned and looked at us. I groaned.

"Look," I whispered. I used the white crayon. I wrote *Hi* on the white paper. "Read the secret message," I said.

Janie frowned. "I can't. I can't see anything."

12

"Right," I said. I used the marker. I colored all over the page. We saw the word *Hi* in big white letters.

"Wow!" Janie said. "That's super, Marshal Matt! We can write secret messages. This will help find my gloves."

I gave a crayon, marker, and some paper to Janie. Time to solve the mystery!

Janie put Blinky in his cage. Blinky flapped his wings. "I'm in jail!" he squawked. Janie giggled. Then she headed to the pond with Fred. Heather and Pam went with her. They wore ice skates too.

I, Marshal Matt, started to search the barn. I needed clues. Fast. Before Janie's fingers froze.

I searched near the hay. I searched near the sleds. I searched the whole barn. No gloves and no clues. I needed help. I needed Mister E!

I walked over to Mister E. I knew he'd been looking too. For the gloves.

"Have you seen gloves with snowmen?" I asked.

Mister E wiggled his right ear. That's how he says yes. Then he pointed with both ears.

I looked where he was pointing. Becky! Becky was holding her sled. On her hands were gloves. Gloves with snowmen!

"Good job," I said. I fed Mister E another carrot. Then I ran over to Becky.

"Nice gloves," I said. "Nice snowmen."

"Thanks, Marshal Matt," Becky giggled. "The gloves were on sale at the store."

"On sale?" I asked.

"Sure," Becky said. "Didn't you know? Everyone got some. Aren't they great?" She wiggled her little fingers. "The snowmen on the end wear blue hats."

Blue hats! Janie's wore red. Matching gloves—almost. The wrong matching gloves. This mystery was harder to solve than I thought.

"We're going sled riding," Becky said. "Want to come?"

"Sure." I got a sled. Time to look for more clues.

A bunch of us headed outside. Into the cold. Into the snow. Our boots slipped on the snow. The snow blew in our faces. *Br-r-r-r!*

We hiked up a big hill. *Huff, huff, puff.* We got to the top. Becky went first. *Whoosh!* She slid down the hill on her sled. Everyone cheered! Hip, hip, hooray!

Everyone took turns. I,
Marshal Matt, looked around. For
clues. All I found was snow.

Suddenly, Pam came running
up the hill. Pam always runs. She
likes to run. She even runs in races.

Pam ran up to me. She gave
me a white piece of paper. Then
Pam hopped on her sled. She held
on with her gloves. I looked at her
gloves. Snowmen! Pam flew down
the hill.

The chase was on! I stuffed the
paper in my pocket. I jumped on
my sled. *Whe-e-e-e!* Down the hill I
raced. *Crash!* I hit a bump and flew

off my sled. I landed in the snow.

"Are you all right, Marshal Matt?" Pam yelled. She ran over. She reached out her hand. She helped me up.

"Mime fime," I said, trying to speak. I wiped the snow off my mouth. "I'm fine. Thanks." I looked at Pam's gloves. "Nice gloves," I said. "Nice snowmen."

"Thanks," Pam giggled. "Aren't they great?" She wiggled her little fingers. "These snowmen wear green hats."

Green hats! Janie's wore red. Matching gloves—almost. Wrong gloves again! And still no clues.

Just then I heard bells. Were
my ears ringing? From my fall? The
bells got louder. I rubbed my ears.
More bells!

"Do you hear bells?" I asked.

"Sure," Pam said. "Sleigh bells.
Here comes Mister E. With the
sleigh!"

Mister E neighed. He was happy to see me. He stopped. Dan and Ben hopped off the sleigh.

I fed Mister E a carrot. "Any clues?" I whispered.

Mister E wiggled his right ear. Yes! He pointed his ears to the left. I looked where he was pointing. Dan!

Dan held out a white piece of paper. Suddenly I remembered! The paper from Pam! Clues?

I got my marker. I colored all over the paper from Pam. I saw the secret message from Janie: *I looked at the pond. My gloves are not at the pond.*

I colored all over the paper from Dan. I saw the second message from Janie: *My fingers are starting to freeze.*

I, Marshal Matt, had two secret messages. But still no clues! And now Janie was in trouble! Her fingers were freezing! I said a quick prayer. I asked Jesus to help Janie not get frozen fingers.

I stuffed the papers into my pockets. I shook Pam's glove. "Thanks for the help."

I turned to Dan. "Thanks for the help." I shook Dan's hand. His cold hand. His cold, bare hand. "Where are your gloves?" I asked.

"I shared them," he said. "I gave them to Janie. Her fingers were freezing." Dan rubbed his hands together. "*Br-r-r-r,*" he said.

"Now *my* fingers are freezing."

"Here, Dan," Ben said. "You can wear my gloves." Ben pulled off his gloves. He gave them to Dan.

"Thanks," Dan said.

Beep, beep, beep, beep. What was that? A clue?

Ben held up his arm. "My watch alarm," he said. "It's time for the snowman contest. Who wants to come?"

"I do! I do!" everyone shouted. Everyone jumped into the sleigh. I climbed in too. Time to look for more clues!

We rode to the barn. Everyone hopped off the sleigh.

Next to the barn stood four snowmen. Janie worked on one. It looked nice. Janie always tries to make things look nice.

Fred helped. He hammered the snow. With his toy hammer.

"I'll help too!" Ben said.

"Thanks," Janie said. "But we have to hurry. It's time for the contest." She stuck two stones in for eyes. I stuck a carrot in for the nose. "Super!" Janie grinned.

Ben put on more snow. Fred hammered it. Ben rubbed his hands together. *"Br-r-r-r! My fingers are freezing!"*

I thought about the Bible verse in my pocket. I thought about sharing. About how many things Jesus shared with me. Even His life—to pay for the bad things I do. "Here, Ben," I said. I tugged off my gloves. "You can wear mine."

"Thanks," Ben said.

They finished the snowman. I looked around for clues. I looked on the ground. Lots of snow. No gloves.

Heather worked on a
snowman. It stood tall and straight.

It had sticks for arms. It wore a tall black hat. It had gloves for hands. Gloves!

This time I looked closer. At the little fingers. The snowmen wore red hats! The mystery was solved!

"Janie's gloves," I said. I pointed to the snowman.

Heather frowned. "*My* gloves," she said.

"Are you sure?" I asked.

"Sure I'm sure," Heather said. "I got them on sale. The snowmen on the little fingers wear red hats. They match Janie's, but they're not hers. They're mine."

I, Marshal Matt, was stumped.
Too many matching gloves. I had
never lost a case before. But this
one was too hard. And now *my*
fingers were freezing. *Br-r-r-r!*

I headed for the barn.
Everyone was inside.

Janie walked up. Blinky sat on
her shoulder.

"No gloves?" she asked.

"There are too many gloves. This case is too hard." I rubbed my hands together. "And now my fingers are freezing!"

Blinky blinked. "Freezing, sneezing!" He sneezed.

Heather walked up. "Wear my gloves, Marshal Matt."

"Thanks for sharing," I said. I pulled on the gloves. "And thanks for helping solve the mystery."

Heather looked surprised. "How did I help?"

Janie looked surprised. "I thought this case was too hard to solve."

"Not anymore," I said. "The mystery is solved."

"But where are my gloves?" Janie pointed to my hands. "Those are Heather's."

"Follow me," I said. Janie and Heather followed me. We headed outside.

A crowd stood around the snowmen. Rich announced the winner. Heather won! Her snowman now wore a blue ribbon. With its hat and gloves.

I wiggled my fingers. The snowmen wiggled on the gloves. I said, "Heather went ice skating too. When she tied on her skates, she took off her gloves."

"That's right," Heather said. She nodded her head.

"Heather put her gloves in her pockets. But she forgot. She saw Janie's on the hay. She thought they were hers. She put on Janie's gloves. Then she hiked to the pond."

"But how do you know?" Janie asked. "For sure?"

I, Marshal Matt, told the rest of
the story. "Heather made a
snowman. She took off Janie's
gloves. She put them on the
snowman."

We looked at the snowman. It
was wearing gloves.

"Later, her hands got cold.
Without thinking, she reached into
her pockets. She found her gloves
and put them on. Then she finished
the snowman."

I held up my hands. I wiggled my fingers again. "Then Heather shared her gloves with me. See? Gloves on the snowman and gloves on me. Matching gloves!"

Just then, someone rang a bell.

Blinky blinked. "Fire! Fire!" he squawked.

"Pizza!" everyone shouted. "It's time for the pizza!"

Janie and Heather giggled. They took Janie's gloves off the snowman. I gave Heather back her gloves. "Thanks!" they shouted and ran into the barn. For pizza.

I, Marshal Matt, grinned. I like pizza best. Especially right after I solve a mystery.

Hey, kids! Join me in my Marshal Matt Cowpoke Club! Remember: You're special! God loves you so much, He sent His Son, Jesus, to die for you. He will help you be an unselfish cowpoke who shares. You can solve mysteries with me! Just write your name on the blank.

With Jesus' help,

I, _____ ,

will be an unselfish member
of the Marshal Matt
Cowpoke Club.

As a member of my club, you can make your very own Marshal Matt secret messages! Turn the page to find out how.

To make your Marshal Matt secret messages you need a white crayon, white paper, and a dark felt-tipped marker.

Write your message on the white paper with white crayon. Share the message with a friend. Ask the friend to color all over the paper with the marker. See how the message suddenly appears?

Write happy messages to your family and friends. Hide the messages where they will find them. Then share your marker and watch them grin!

And remember: God knows you're special, and I do too!

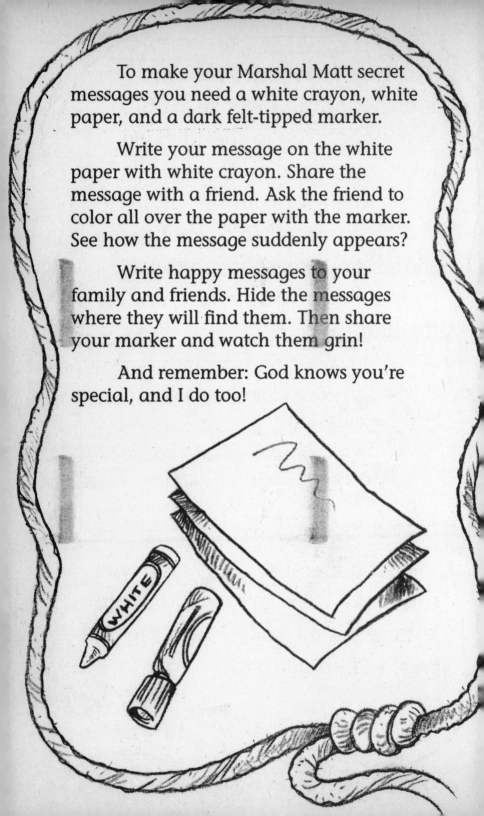